Desert Ordeal

BY

Ed Hanson

THE BARCLAY FAMILY ADVENTURES

Development and Production: Laurel Associates, Inc.
Cover and Interior Art: Black Eagle Productions

SADDLEBACK
PUBLISHING·INC.
Three Watson
Irvine, CA 92618-2767

Website: www.sdlback.com

ISBN 1-56254-552-3

Printed in the United States of America
08 07 06 05   9 8 7 6 5 4 3 2 1

CONTENTS

MEET THE BARCLAYS

Paul Barclay
A fun-loving father of three who takes his kids on his travels whenever he can.

Ann Barclay
The devoted mother who manages the homefront during Paul's many absences as an on-site construction engineer.

Jim Barclay
The eldest child, Jim is a talented athlete with his eye on a football scholarship at a major college.

Aaron Barclay
Three years younger than Jim, he's inquisitive, daring, and an absolute whiz in science class.

Pam Barclay
Adopted from Korea as a baby, Pam is a spunky middle-schooler who more than holds her own with her lively older brothers.

CHAPTER 1

Heading West

Paul Barclay picked up the phone on the third ring. He'd just come back from a job in Canada and was looking forward to some time off. On-site construction engineers worked long hours. And Paul had been missing his family back in Rockdale. Another assignment right now was the *last* thing he wanted!

"Hello," Paul said.

"Is this Paul Barclay?" said the voice on the other end of the line.

"Yes, it is," Paul answered.

"This is Norman Wheeler, Mr. Barclay. I'm president of Consolidated Industries in California. My company is planning a major expansion of our plant here. I've been told you're just the man to help us design the whole project and oversee its construction."

Paul paused and thought for a moment.

"That's very flattering, Mr. Wheeler. But I've just finished a long, tiring job. The truth is, I was looking forward to a little vacation time."

"Not a problem, Mr. Barclay. We can't start for six to eight weeks anyway. The only thing is—I'd like you to come out here in the next few days. Just to look at the job, you know. If you agree to take it on, we can come to terms. Then you can take your vacation before you start work."

Paul thought it over for a moment. "Well, okay, Mr. Wheeler, I suppose I can do that," he responded.

"Great! I can send our company plane to pick you up. That way you won't have to deal with the airlines. How does that sound, Mr. Barclay?"

"Mr. Wheeler, I've been talking about taking my three children to California for some time now. Would your plane be large enough to handle the four of us?" Paul asked.

"That won't be a problem at all. Our plane's an eight-passenger Beechcraft," Mr. Wheeler explained. "Your kids will be welcome. Oh—and just one more thing, Mr. Barclay."

"What's that?" Paul asked.

"Don't be surprised when you see our pilot," Mr. Wheeler answered.

"Why do you say that?" Paul asked.

"Because he doesn't exactly look or dress like a traditional pilot. The man's name is Johnny Hightower. He's a Native American—a member of the Navajo tribe, I believe," Mr. Wheeler answered.

"I don't care anything about that.

My one and only concern is that he's a good aviator," Paul said.

"Oh, he's a good pilot, all right. In fact, he's one of the best!" Mr. Wheeler answered just before hanging up.

Two days later, Paul, Jim, Aaron, and Pam were waiting at the private plane section of the airport. From behind them, they heard a voice say, "This must be the Barclay family!"

They all turned at once. Before them stood a big, burly man, well over six feet tall and weighing about 225 pounds. His long, dark hair was tied back in a ponytail. He was wearing a bolo tie, a checkered western shirt, blue jeans, and boots.

"Hello, there! My name is Johnny Hightower. But you folks can call me Johnny—everybody does."

"Hi, Johnny. I'm Paul Barclay."

Johnny reached out and shook Paul's hand warmly.

"And these are my three children—Jim, Aaron, and Pam," Paul said.

Pam looked up at the pilot eagerly. "Hi! Where's our airplane, Johnny?" she asked.

"Right over there," Johnny answered.

He pointed at a sleek silver plane standing about 50 yards to the left.

Pam looked a bit disappointed. "Gee," she said, "it looks kind of small."

Paul laughed at the expression on Pam's face. "You've been spoiled by too many trips in big jets, young lady!"

The little group walked over to the plane. Johnny opened the big storage compartment. Jim helped him stow the Barclays' luggage inside. Then Paul and his excited kids boarded the plane. In a few minutes, they were in their seats, awaiting takeoff.

Ten minutes later they were in the air. They watched the city spread out below them. Johnny Hightower leveled the plane out at their cruising altitude and switched onto automatic pilot.

Then he turned to Paul and said, "This is really a great plane. It will almost fly itself."

Several hours later, Paul noticed that the sky was darkening up ahead. He turned to Johnny and saw a concerned look on the pilot's face.

"What is it, Johnny?" Paul asked.

"I'm afraid we're in for some rough weather, Paul. Looks like a big storm up ahead. Thunderclouds extend for miles to our left and right—so we can't go around it. A big jet might be able to climb above the storm, but this plane can't fly that high."

Just minutes later, the small plane disappeared into the thick, dark clouds.

CHAPTER 2

Forced Landing

Sheets of rain streaked down the windows. Over the hum of the engine, the Barclays could see jagged flashes of lightning and hear loud claps of thunder. Then the little plane started to rock violently in the heavy winds. It shook so hard, in fact, that Aaron wondered if a wing might fall off!

Then it happened. A loud clap of thunder and a lightning flash lit up the sky. The Beechcraft shuddered as Johnny struggled to keep it under control.

"Oh, no! That last bolt of lightning hit us!" Johnny yelled.

As he spoke, the steady hum of the engine came to an abrupt stop.

"Can you radio our position?" Paul

shouted over the roar of the storm.

"Can't do that, I'm afraid. The radio is gone, too."

For the next five minutes, Johnny struggled with the controls. Then, as suddenly as it had started, the storm was over. The plane was now out of the dark cloud mass and the sun was shining. But with no power, the little Beechcraft was rapidly losing altitude.

There was an eerie quiet inside the cabin now. The only sound was the air whipping past the windshield and around the wings.

Paul looked at Johnny. He saw that the pilot was fighting hard to keep control of the powerless plane. "Can we make it?" he whispered.

"Well, we're going to have to make a forced landing," Johnny answered. "But the good news is that we're out of the storm and over the desert."

Paul looked out the window. The ground below looked *very* far away.

"A crash landing is fairly easy in the desert," Johnny continued. "There are no trees to hit, and the ground surface is pretty flat. But our landing will probably be a little bumpy, Paul. So, make sure the kids are buckled in real tight."

Paul turned toward his children. When he told them to tighten their seat belts, he could see the fear in their eyes. But they didn't say a word as the desert below them rapidly got closer and closer.

"*Brace yourselves!*" Johnny yelled.

The tail section hit the desert floor first. It skidded for a hundred yards or so before the nose came down. A great cloud of sand flew over the plane. Before coming to a complete stop, the little Beechcraft slid along the flat desert floor for several hundred more feet.

For a few seconds, there was an eerie silence. Then everyone breathed a deep sigh of relief.

Finally, Paul looked around and said,

"Is everyone all right?"

One by one the kids answered.

"I'm okay," Jim called out.

"I'm all right, too, Dad," Aaron replied in a shaky voice.

"I guess I'm okay—but I'm still scared," Pam piped up.

"You have every right to be scared," Paul said soothingly. "Crash-landing in a desert is *not* a lot of fun."

Paul turned to Johnny Hightower. The expression on the pilot's face was still calm and composed.

"Congratulations! You did a heck of a good job bringing the plane down safely, Johnny."

"Thanks a lot," Johnny replied. "We're really lucky that we were over the desert and not a heavily wooded area."

Jim looked around the vast, barren desert. "What do we do now?" he asked.

Johnny thought for a moment.

"First, let's take an inventory of what we have onboard in the way of supplies.

We may be stuck here for a day or two, so food and water will be important— particularly water," Johnny replied.

Jim tried to open the door near the cockpit, but it wouldn't budge.

"Maybe the doorframe bent a little," Paul said. "Let's both try it."

With two of them pushing on the door, it quickly flew open. Sand poured into the cabin. As they climbed out of the plane, they were struck by how hot and dry the air was. Under the blazing sun, the sand was hot to the touch.

"Whew! It must be 100 degrees out here," Aaron said.

"Maybe more," Johnny answered. "But don't worry. The desert always cools off at night. The important thing in the daytime is to stay covered and protect your bodies from the sun."

They slowly took everything useful out of the plane. They found a toolbox, a first aid kit, a small hatchet, and four blankets. Between them they had a few candy bars, some little packages of peanuts, and one peanut butter and jelly sandwich that Pam had brought along with her.

"That doesn't look like much food," Aaron said.

"Food won't be our biggest problem, kids," Johnny said.

Then he shaded his eyes and stared out to the north.

"What are you looking at?" Paul asked.

"Do you see those hills to the north? I figure they must be about three miles away—four at the most. We should be able to find a water hole up there," Johnny replied.

"But shouldn't we stay close to the plane?" Jim asked.

"Good point," Johnny said. "That's our best chance of rescue. But if we leave before sun up, we can be back to the plane before noon. I think it's our only choice. We may be here for days—and we *must* have water to drink."

"Okay, Johnny. We'll be ready to head out at first light," Paul agreed.

That evening the little group of travelers wrapped up in blankets and huddled under the plane. Johnny had been right. As soon as the sun went down, there was a definite chill in the desert air.

"If this had to happen," Pam said bravely, "I'm glad we have someone with us who knows all about the desert."

Johnny threw back his head and laughed. "I hate to disappoint you, little one—but I was raised in San Francisco. Now, if my famous great-grandfather Billy Two Nose was here, that would be different!"

"How on earth did he get a name like Billy Two Nose?" Aaron asked.

"Oh, that's a long story," Johnny said with a grin. He tightened his blanket around his shoulders. "But then—we aren't going anywhere, are we?"

CHAPTER 3

Billy Two Nose

"Way back in my great-grandfather's day," Johnny explained, "the American desert was a far different place than it is now. In those days, Indian villages dotted all the deserts in Arizona, Utah, and New Mexico.

"The Navajos, my great-grandfather Billy's tribe, were basically farmers and herders. They fought when attacked, but they weren't warlike by nature.

"The other major desert tribe was the Apaches. They were fierce warriors and a nomadic people who kept on the move.

"Billy grew up in a small village. He became well-known for one amazing ability. He could *sense* things before they happened! By the time he was 16 years old, the other people in the village thought that Billy had some sort of gift. Today, you'd call it ESP, I guess.

"Anyway, as the story goes, it was early afternoon on a spring day when Billy was staring out into the desert. He couldn't see anything—but he somehow sensed great danger to the village!

"They say he rushed through the camp, telling the women and children to hide in the nearby hills. Then he had all the men arm themselves to prepare for battle. I'm sure that some people must have thought he was crazy. But his reputation for seeing things in advance made them do as he asked.

"An hour or so later, nothing at all had happened. The men started to grumble and complain. Then, just as they were about to return to their normal routines, a huge cloud of dust appeared on the horizon.

"As the cloud got closer, the Navajos could make out riders in war paint. A raiding party of armed Apaches was thundering toward them! It was clear they intended to loot the Navajo village.

"The Apaches rode into camp, expecting to find the villagers tending cattle and planting crops. They thought there would be little resistance to their surprise raid. Instead, the Apaches were the ones who were surprised.

"The Navajo arrows found their mark. In the first 20 minutes, half of the Apache raiding party was killed. The whole battle lasted less than an hour. What was left of the Apaches retreated across the desert, leaving their dead behind. But only two Navajos had been injured—and none were killed!

"Billy was a hero. The Navajos held a feast in his honor that evening. One of the tribal elders said, 'A man with just one nose couldn't smell out trouble like

Billy does!' So that evening he was given the name Billy Two Nose. That special name stuck with him the rest of his life."

"That's a great story, Johnny!" Aaron cried out in delight.

"Yeah," Johnny answered. "It's one of the favorite old stories that Navajos pass down from generation to generation."

Paul yawned. "We're going to have quite a hike tomorrow, kids. We'd better get some sleep."

It had been an exhausting day for all of them. Stranded in the desert or not, sleep came easily.

CHAPTER 4

Trip to the Mountains

It was 5 o'clock the next morning when Johnny and the Barclays started their trek to the mountains. The sun wouldn't peek over the horizon for at least another hour. The air was still chilly. But everyone knew that once the desert sun came up, the weather would warm up fast.

There were no suitable containers on the plane to use as water jugs. But the seat cushions were enveloped in airtight plastic covers. Johnny carefully removed two of the covers.

He figured they could carry three or four quarts of water in each one.

Certainly, that should provide plenty of water for the five of them until they were rescued.

Taking the lead, Johnny Hightower set a brisk pace. He hoped to be in the mountains before the sun rose too high in the eastern sky.

Every five minutes or so, he'd look back to see how the others were doing. When he saw that everyone was keeping up, he maintained his brisk pace.

One hour later they reached the base of the mountain. Johnny turned to the Barclays and smiled.

"Good work, guys," he said. "Let's take a five-minute rest now."

No one complained. After an hour of speed-walking, they all appreciated the break. Jim sat down on a rock and rubbed his aching feet.

He looked worried. "What if we can't find water?" he asked.

"Then we'll be very thirsty," Johnny

answered. "But I'm almost *sure* that we can find water somewhere up there!"

"I hope you're right," Pam said. "I'm pretty thirsty right now."

"Well, let's get started, then. The sooner we get up there, the sooner we can get a nice, cool drink," Johnny said.

The five hikers had climbed for 20 minutes when Aaron spoke up.

"I think you're right, Johnny. We *should* find water up here," he said.

Paul smiled. "What makes you so sure of that, son?" he asked.

"It's easy, Dad. All living things need water to survive. So far, I've seen a rabbit, a ground squirrel, some birds, and a bunch of insects. They must be getting water somewhere!"

Johnny nodded and smiled.

"Good thinking, Aaron," he said. "Let's spread out a bit and take a look around. Don't go too far, though. We don't want anyone getting lost."

From about 100 feet up, they looked down on the vast desert below. Now their plane was only a speck, miles to the south. The desert seemed to go on forever, like an endless sea of sand.

Jim took his sister in tow.

"Come walk along with me, Sis," he said. "You always bring me luck."

They decided to climb up to a rocky area off to their left. It was Pam who found the small spring. Sure enough, pure, fresh water was bubbling out of a rock formation! A loud yell brought everyone running up to her and Jim.

After they all took turns drinking, Johnny carefully filled both plastic bags. He gave Paul one bag to carry, and he took the other. It was only 9 o'clock when they started back down the mountain.

"With any luck," Johnny said, "we should be back at the plane shortly before noon."

CHAPTER 5

Sandstorm

The return trip was a little slower. Paul and Johnny had to be very careful not to spill their precious cargo.

When they finally reached the base of the mountain, they rested before starting out across the desert. Now, the sun was high in the sky, and the temperature was rising rapidly.

They'd walked about half an hour when a concerned look came over Johnny's face. He stopped walking and stood staring off to the west.

The Barclays looked across the desert, too—but they couldn't see anything. Nothing but an occasional sand dune or a big cactus broke up the flatness of the desert floor.

Johnny turned back to the Barclays. Paul noticed the anxious look in his eyes.

"We have to get back to the plane as quickly as possible," he said.

"Why? What is it, Johnny?" Paul asked quietly. "What's the matter?"

"Looks like a sandstorm is coming," he answered. "And that isn't something we want to get caught in—especially out in the open."

All five of them started running ahead. Now their downed plane was barely visible. Johnny guessed that it was still a mile or so ahead of them.

A few minutes later Paul looked back to the west again. Now he could see a dark, black cloud rolling across the desert floor. The cloud was five or six miles to the west—but it was closing in fast!

Paul and Johnny were worried. If they tried to move too fast, they could easily spill the water they were carrying.

They almost made it. When the plane was only a few hundred yards away, the first gusts of wind hit them. Suddenly, sand started to pelt their skin with great force. The blast of gritty particles felt as sharp as needles!

Breathing became more difficult. The wind-blown sand flew up their nostrils! Speech was impossible.

Johnny and the Barclays stumbled ahead blindly. Keeping their eyes open was too painful to even consider.

"Okay—I want each of you to hold onto the person in front of you," Johnny instructed. "Whatever you do, *stay together!*" With visibility down to a few feet, getting separated from the group could mean disaster. Luckily, they reached the plane and climbed inside just as the full force of the storm hit.

The little Beechcraft rocked and shuddered in the wind. The pinging sound of sand and small pebbles bouncing off the metal hull soon became deafening. Visibility dropped to zero as the air thickened with sand and other desert debris.

Pam peered out the window.

"Gosh, I'm glad we aren't out there right now!" she said.

"Me, too. Plain old sand can be very dangerous under these conditions," Johnny answered solemnly.

Aaron looked at Johnny curiously. "How did you know that a sandstorm was coming? There was nothing to see."

Johnny shook his head.

"I really don't know," he replied. "I just sort of *felt* it, I guess."

Jim laughed. "You must have some of your great-grandfather's talents," he said. "Maybe we should start calling *you* Johnny Two Nose."

In spite of the storm, Jim's comment gave all of them a good laugh.

CHAPTER 6

Night Visitors

It was late afternoon before the storm finally passed. Paul struggled to push open the hatch and then stepped out to look around. The desert looked about the same—but the Beechcraft was almost buried in sand.

Now Johnny climbed down. He glanced at the plane and said, "No one will ever see us under all this sand. We'll have to clean it all off if we want to be visible from the air."

Johnny had scarcely finished his sentence when the faint drone of an airplane engine sounded overhead. Five pairs of anxious eyes scanned the sky to the south.

"*I see it!*" Jim yelled.

Aaron looked doubtful.

"Yes—but will they see *us*?" he asked.

"Right. They may not with the plane all buried deep in the sand," Johnny answered. "That's why it's important that we clean it off."

They were disappointed when the high-flying aircraft passed miles south of them. Paul tried to cheer up the kids.

"Don't worry," he said. "There are sure to be other planes looking for us."

"But I was so sure we'd be rescued by now!" Pam said quietly.

"Remember, little one," Johnny said, "our radio went out. I couldn't signal our position. The storm probably blew us miles off our flight plan.

"That means that a rescue plane has to search a very large area. But I promise that they *will* find us!"

As the sun set in the west, they all worked to clean off the plane. It was a big job, but gradually the silver body of the Beechcraft reappeared.

Paul looked at the plane's sleek surface. "Well," he said, "that should shine in tomorrow's sun. We should be visible for miles."

Johnny agreed.

"I hope you're right," Pam said.

The hard work had made everyone thirsty. Johnny gave one cup of their precious water to each person.

"I know you'd like to drink more, but we have to ration our water. We don't want to make another trip to the mountains, do we?" he asked.

It was dark now, and they were dead tired. The trip to the mountains, the race to beat the approaching sandstorm, and the hard work of cleaning the plane had taken their toll.

Everyone decided to sleep outside again in the soft sand. They all had their blankets if it got too cool.

Just before they dozed off, Aaron said, "Gee, wouldn't a big, ol' pizza taste good right now?"

"Darn you, Aaron!" Pam cried out. "Don't even *talk* about food. Until now I had forgotten how hungry I was."

"Maybe I can get us something to eat tomorrow," Johnny offered.

"What would that be?" Pam asked.

"Some cactus plants have a pulp that's fairly nourishing. The taste is kind of bitter—but it will give you energy and keep up your strength. In the morning I'll see if I can find some."

In the middle of the night, Paul suddenly awoke from a sound sleep. He thought he'd heard something moving around the plane.

He stared out into the blackness. There was that sound again! And now he was certain that he could see something moving 25 to 30 yards away. He shook Johnny's shoulder.

"Wake up, Johnny," he whispered. "I don't know what it is—but there's something moving around out there."

Johnny sat up and listened.

After a moment, he said, "We'd better move the kids inside the plane."

Paul was alarmed.

"Why?" he asked. "What is it?"

"I think it may be a pack of coyotes. They usually stay clear of humans. But they've been known to attack if they're hungry enough. And this pack is a little too close for comfort!"

CHAPTER 7

Den of Snakes

Johnny woke up just as the sun was rising. He quietly pushed open the hatch and stepped out of the plane. He wanted to check the sand for tracks. Then he could determine how large the coyote pack was and how close it had come to the plane.

He saw the first tracks only 15 yards away. After studying the ground, he figured there must have been at least a dozen animals in the group. Then the hatch door opened and Paul stepped out. He walked over to Johnny.

"Morning, Johnny. Well, how about it? Was it coyotes?" he asked.

"I'm afraid so. A pack of about a

dozen of them, I figure. The poor things must be nearly starving to be so brazen. Usually, coyotes won't come within 100 yards of humans."

Paul frowned. "Is there a chance they could attack us?" he asked.

"Not during the day. The desert sun is much too hot for them. But after dark, we'd better be careful from now on," Johnny replied.

"Let's not say anything about this to the kids, Johnny. I don't want to give them anything else to worry about."

Johnny nodded his head and smiled. "Whatever you say, Paul," he replied. "Father knows best."

Yawning and stretching, Jim, Aaron, and Pam climbed down from the plane a few minutes later. Paul and Johnny walked over to them.

"I'm hungry! Do you think we're going to find some cactus pulp to eat today?" Jim asked.

"Sure," Johnny answered. "There are a couple of important things we need to do today. First, you boys and I will take a hike. Let's see if we can find an edible cactus plant."

Pam felt left out. "What about Dad and me?" she asked.

"I suggest that you two work at pulling anything out of the plane that we can burn. Make a big pile of stuff, if you can. Then we can light it when we hear or see a plane coming. A big smoke cloud is visible for miles and miles. It's probably our best chance at rescue."

"Good idea, Johnny," Paul said. "We can also try to siphon a little gas out of the plane. When the time comes, that will help us get a good fire going."

"Okay, Paul. The boys and I will get going now. We'll see you back here in a couple of hours," Johnny said.

Johnny took the hatchet. Then he and Jim and Aaron started out across the desert. About 40 minutes later, Johnny spied a large cactus plant.

"That's just what I was looking for!" he cried out happily.

He hacked away with the hatchet until he had three large pieces. He and the boys each took a piece and started back toward the plane.

Their spirits were surprisingly high. The boys had slept well the night before. And—despite being hungry—they still felt excited and challenged by their adventure in the desert.

Aaron was 15 yards ahead of Johnny and Jim when he looked back to say something. Paying little attention to where he was going, he didn't see the deep gully that stretched across his path. While looking over his shoulder, he stumbled and fell into the ravine!

Thankfully, Aaron was dazed but unhurt. He smiled up at them from the bottom of the gully. He was about to make a joke about his clumsiness. But then a distinctive sound brought a shudder of fear to his heart. It was the unmistakable clicking of a rattlesnake!

Eight feet overhead, Johnny and Jim were staring down at Aaron from the top of the gully.

"Aaron! Are you all right?" Jim called down to his brother.

Aaron's eyes were huge and his mouth was hanging open. He was staring at a group of diamondback snakes on a rocky shelf. His shock had now turned to panic. Their peaceful slumber disturbed, the agitated snakes started to wriggle around. Several appeared to be coiled to strike, their rattles clicking noisily. Others were moving out into the open to get a closer look at their unwanted guest.

"There are rattlesnakes down here!" Aaron shouted as he frantically jumped to his feet.

The snakes were just a few yards away from him! Johnny leaned into the gully and lowered his hand.

"Jump up and grab my hand, Aaron!" he shouted.

Aaron took two quick steps and bent his knees. But just as he was about to make a leap, a six-foot diamondback struck his leg!

A sharp pain shot through his thigh. He watched in horror as the fangs pierced his pantleg and injected deadly venom into his flesh! The boy was crying out in fear and pain as Johnny finally pulled him up.

"One of the rattlers bit me!" he said. "Am I going to die?"

"No, Aaron, you won't die! Just stay calm and don't move around. Physical activity only speeds up the venom's movement in the body."

Johnny turned to Jim.

"Get back to the plane as fast as you

can, Jim," he said quietly. "In the box of medical supplies, you'll find a snakebite kit with anti-venom. Get it back here as fast as you can. Your brother's life depends on it!"

Chapter 8

Rush to Safety

Jim was in good shape. Jogging effortlessly, he headed out across the desert. He figured that it was about a mile back to the plane. But under the hot sun, he knew he'd have to pace himself carefully.

Johnny watched Jim disappear in the distance. Then he tried to make the frightened boy as comfortable as possible. Cradling Aaron's head in his lap, he shielded him from the sun with his own body.

"Just try to lie quietly, Aaron. Jim will be back before long. When we get the anti-venom into your system, you'll feel much better."

"Okay, Johnny," Aaron answered. "I don't feel much like moving around anyway." Then he added, "Aren't we supposed to make a cut near the bite and suck the poison out?"

"You've been watching too many old movies, son," Johnny said with a smile. "That treatment fell out of favor years ago. The anti-venom serum is your best bet—although you may not have much interest in horseback riding after this."

"What do you mean by that?"

"The anti-venom comes from horses. Antibodies are created when a horse is injected with snake venom," Johnny explained. "When the serum is injected into people, they sometimes develop an allergy to horses.

"But it may not affect you that way," Johnny continued in a calming voice. "Everyone is different. But even if it does—it's a small price to pay for neutralizing the snake venom."

Beads of sweat were now running down Aaron's face, and his pulse rate had increased. Despite all of Johnny's efforts to keep Aaron still, the poison was flowing through his young body.

Back at the plane, Pam was surprised to see Jim jogging toward her.

"Dad!" she cried. "Here's Jim! And he's all alone!"

Paul knew at once that something must have gone wrong.

"What's the matter, Jim?" he asked.

"Aaron's been bitten by a rattler. Where's the first aid box? I need to get right back with the anti-venom."

Paul's face went pale.

"How far away are they?" he asked.

"About a mile," Jim answered as he grabbed the snakebite kit and headed back out across the desert.

"Come on, Pam," Paul said as he picked up one of the water bags. "We'll go out to meet them."

Precious minutes were ticking by as Johnny stared in the direction of the plane. At last he saw a figure coming into view. When Jim finally handed off the snakebite kit to Johnny, he was breathing hard and soaked with sweat.

Johnny lost no time. He quickly removed the anti-venom syringe and injected the serum into Aaron. He looked at his watch. Good! It had been only 20 minutes since the boy had been bitten.

"You did a fine job getting back here so quickly, Jim. Your brother should start to feel better real soon."

Johnny carefully lifted Aaron up onto his shoulders. Then the three of them started back in the direction of the plane. It was very slow going under the blazing desert sun. In about five minutes, they saw Paul and Pam heading toward them.

Paul ran up to Johnny. "How is he?"

he asked with a worried look on his face.

"Thanks to Jim, he's going to be just fine," Johnny replied. "He may feel a little dizzy for a while, but he'll be up and around by tomorrow."

Aaron looked up at his dad. He was *already* starting to feel a little better! He smiled weakly and clutched Paul's hand.

"I guess I'd better look where I'm going from now on," he said.

"It wouldn't be a bad idea, son," Paul said as he gave his son a big hug.

Pam held out the water bag.

"Look what I brought. Does anyone want a drink?" she asked.

In two minutes, the plastic water bag was empty!

CHAPTER 9

Becoming More Visible

Back at the plane, Paul did his best to make Aaron comfortable. He rigged a sandy bed for him in the shade under the wing. He cleaned the bite wound on the boy's leg and applied a bandage. Pam sat next to her brother, talking to him until he fell asleep.

Johnny knew that the other kids were concerned about Aaron. He tried as hard as he could to reassure them.

"Don't worry. He should be just fine. Keeping him still and getting the antivenom into him after just 20 minutes was crucial," he said.

While Aaron lay sleeping, the others

continued to prepare the bonfire. Paul was able to draw a little gasoline from the plane. Now, when the time came, lighting a big fire should be no problem.

Since it was already late afternoon, they decided to wait until the next morning to light the fire. If they could keep it burning most of the day, they had high hopes that someone would spot the smoke.

The little group sat under the plane, munching on chunks of cactus.

"I know this isn't as good as sirloin steak," Johnny said, laughing. "But, believe it or not, it's better than some of the food our troops ate during the war."

"Did you serve in the armed forces? Tell us about it," Jim said.

"Yeah—but that was long after World War II. My father was a radioman on the island of Bataan in 1942, though. He saw plenty of action."

"Wasn't that the year that Bataan fell

to the Japanese forces?" Paul asked.

"You're right, Paul. Our troops were badly outnumbered. And they were all out of food, medicine, and ammo. They had been driven to the southern tip of the island with the sea at their backs.

"They had no hope of receiving additional supplies or reinforcements. And even worse, many of our soldiers were sick. Malaria, typhoid, dysentery—you name it, and they had it."

"How awful! What happened to them?" Pam asked.

"Their situation was desperate. In an attempt to save thousands of lives, our forces surrendered. Then the prisoners were marched to a detainment camp some 100 miles to the north.

"My father told me about some of the things they ate to stay alive," Johnny continued. "Rats, insects—even grubs! So I guess we shouldn't do too much complaining about this cactus pulp!"

Jim was impressed.

"As a matter of fact, this cactus is tasting better all the time," he said.

"Tell me something, Johnny," Paul said. "I've read that there was a great demand for Navajos to serve as radiomen in World War II. Is that true?"

"You bet. The Japanese knew many languages—but they didn't know *our* language. That's why my people could relay secret messages without fear of enemy interception."

"What's everybody taking about?" Aaron asked as he opened his eyes.

Paul studied his son's face.

"How are you feeling?" he asked.

"Well, I'd like to try a little of that pulp, if there's any left."

Pam chuckled. "He must be feeling better if he's getting hungry."

"I think maybe we should move inside the plane," Johnny suggested.

"How come?" Jim asked. "It's a lot

more comfortable out here."

"Well, there's something we didn't tell you guys," Paul said. "We had some unexpected visitors last night."

"Huh? What visitors?" all three kids asked at once.

"A pack of coyotes came around here after dark," Paul replied. "Johnny said they can be dangerous when they're hungry."

"Yikes! That reason is plenty good enough for me," Aaron cried out.

In a few moments, everyone was safely inside the plane.

"I have a good feeling that we'll be rescued tomorrow," Johnny said.

Jim studied Johnny's face. "If we are, Johnny, you're getting the name 'Two Nose' for sure."

CHAPTER 10

Coyotes Return

Later that night, the coyotes returned! Somehow they seemed to sense that the people in the plane had no weapons. Having nothing to fear, they approached the plane boldly.

In the bright moonlight, the coyotes were clearly visible. The thin, mangy creatures had angry, red eyes. Their sharp teeth were dripping saliva.

Peering out of the airplane window, Pam said, "I'm sure glad we aren't out there with those things!"

"They don't look very friendly, do they, Buttons?" Paul answered.

"Will they be gone in the morning?" Pam asked hopefully.

"I think so, honey. Johnny said that they don't like the hot sun. They find a shady place to hide during the day."

Johnny was the first one up the next morning. He opened the plane's hatch and stepped down onto the sand. He'd taken just two steps when he heard a frightening growl behind him. Johnny turned and stared in horror. The coyote pack was just a few yards away!

As Johnny leaped back to the safety of the plane, one of the hungry animals made a lunge for his leg. Thankfully, Johnny's quick reaction saved him from a painful bite. The others awoke as he slammed the door of the hatch.

"What is it?" Paul asked.

"We've got a problem," Johnny explained. "Do you remember that I told you the coyotes usually seek shade during the day?"

"Yeah, I remember."

"Well, today they're seeking relief

from the sun in the shade of our plane."

"You mean the whole *pack* is still out there?" Paul gasped.

"I'm afraid so, Paul. And they seem quite content under the wings."

"Oh, no! Then how are we going to get out to light the fire?" Jim asked.

"That's a very good question," said Johnny. "Unless we can figure out a way to drive them off, we aren't!"

For the next two hours or so, they all racked their brains. But no one could think of anything that would scare off the coyote pack.

Aaron, who was feeling much better now, suddenly said, "*Listen!*"

In the quiet that followed, they could hear the faint drone of a distant airplane engine.

"I sure wish we had that fire going now," Johnny said. "But our plane isn't covered with sand anymore. Maybe they'll see us anyway."

"Dad, I think that plane is getting closer," Aaron said excitedly.

Jim listened. "Aaron's right," he said. "That engine noise is *definitely* louder than it was before."

They stared out of the Beechcraft's windows, trying to catch sight of the plane. As they searched the sky with no success, the engine noise began to grow fainter. A sense of despair set in as they realized that the plane was flying away.

But, unknown to them, the grounded Beechcraft *had* been spotted. The pilot of the search plane had radioed their position, and help would soon be on the way!

An hour later, a big helicopter came roaring across the desert. Blowing huge clouds of sand, it circled the Beechcraft several times.

Together, the pelting sand and the engine noise sent the coyotes running for safety. Once the pack was gone, the pilot landed the helicopter about 25 yards away from the Beechcraft.

Johnny and the Barclays climbed out of the plane to greet their rescuers. Jugs of cool, refreshing water were passed around and everyone had long drinks.

Some of the crew members passed out peanut butter sandwiches.

While everyone was eating, Captain Peters said, "I'm really sorry it took us quite so long to find you. We'd been concentrating our search 30 miles south of here."

Johnny smiled. "That's just what I figured had happened," he said. "I knew that the storm had blown us way off of our flight plan."

"Well, the important thing is that you're here now!" Pam said, as she gulped down her second sandwich.

CHAPTER 11

Rescue

Dr. Robert James, a member of the rescue crew, examined Aaron's leg. He pulled up the boy's pantleg and took a close look at the bite that Paul had bandaged.

"What do you think, Doctor?" Paul asked. "Will he be all right?"

"He'll be fine," the doctor answered. "Getting that anti-venom into him so quickly saved his life. And the fact that he's young and healthy was also in his favor."

About 40 or so minutes later, the helicopter was airborne and heading back to its base. Paul spoke to his children as they flew over the desert.

"I want all of you to know how proud I am to be your dad," he said. "I know that you were terribly hungry, thirsty, and uncomfortable—but you didn't complain! I don't think there are many kids who could have handled the last four days as well as you did."

"You're right there," Johnny agreed. "If I ever have to be stranded in the desert again—and I pray that I don't—I hope I'm with the Barclay family."

"Well, thanks, Johnny," Jim said with a grin. "I don't think *any* of us ever wants to go through this again!"

"For once, my big brother is right," Pam laughed. "The next sand I see better be on a beach! So don't plan on *me* ever getting lost in the desert again!"

Spirits were high. The laughing and joking continued for the next hour. Finally, the vast, barren desert gave way to civilization. Now they were looking down on tall buildings. A patchwork of roads spread out below them. Off in the distance, they could see an airport.

Captain Peters landed the helicopter 25 yards from one of the terminal buildings.

Johnny, who was staring out the window, said, "Wow! There's my boss, Mr. Wheeler! I hope he's not mad at me for ditching his plane in the desert."

"I wouldn't worry about that," Paul said. "My guess is that he probably wants to congratulate you for saving all of our lives!"

When the helicopter door opened, Norman Wheeler was the first one to come on board.

"Johnny! Paul! Thank goodness you're all safe! We've been worried sick about you," he said.

"You can thank Johnny for that," Paul answered. "He did a lot more than just make a difficult landing without an engine. He also helped us to survive four long days in the desert heat."

Mr. Wheeler put his hand on Johnny's shoulder. "I told you he was a good pilot," he said before turning back to Paul. "Now, Paul, I want you to know how bad I feel about this accident. I really want to make it up to you somehow."

"No need to, Mr. Wheeler. The storm and the landing in the desert certainly weren't *your* fault," Paul said.

"Even so," Mr. Wheeler continued, "Consolidated Industries wants to pick up all the expenses for the vacation you'd planned. Take as much time as you want. You certainly deserve it. But, first, make sure you and your family are well-rested. In time, this desert ordeal will be just a memory."

"Well, that's very kind of you, Mr. Wheeler," Paul answered.

"There's a rental car waiting for you in the parking lot," Mr. Wheeler said as he tossed Paul a set of car keys.

"Thank you, Mr. Wheeler. We'll take your advice and spend five or six days resting. Then I'll be in touch with you."

Paul walked over to Johnny and gripped his hand firmly.

"I don't think we could have ever made it without you, Johnny. Thanks for everything."

Jim and Aaron were next. They also thanked Johnny and promised never to forget him. Pam reached out and put her arms around the tall Native American. As he leaned down to return her hug, she kissed him on the cheek.

Paul thought he saw tears in Johnny's eyes. Their parting was an emotional time for everyone.

Pam turned back to Johnny just as they were leaving the helicopter. Grinning from ear to ear, she said, "Goodbye now, Johnny Two Nose."

As he waved goodbye to the Barclays,

Norman Wheeler said, "Johnny Two Nose? What does that mean?"

Johnny laughed.

"Oh, it's a long story, Mr. Wheeler," Johnny said with a smile. "I'll have to tell it to you sometime."

COMPREHENSION QUESTIONS

Remembering Details

1. What is Paul Barclay's occupation?

2. What two vital parts of the plane were disabled when lightning hit?

3. What did Johnny say they would need even more than food?

4. Johnny Hightower was a member of which Native American tribe?

5. Why did Johnny lead the Barclays up into the mountains?

6. What kind of nourishing food did the desert provide?

7. What animal attacked Aaron?

8. Why was it important to clear the sand off the downed plane?

Who and Where?

1. What's the name of the Barclays' hometown?

2. What state were the Barclays on their way to visit?

3. Who was the pilot of the company plane?

4. Who found the mountain spring?

5. Who brought the anti-venom serum to Aaron?

6. Who was Johnny Hightower's great-grandfather?

7. Who siphoned gas from the plane's fuel tank?